THIS WALKER BOOK BELONGS TO:

_____

_____

_____

_____

First published 1993 by
Walker Books Ltd
87 Vauxhall Walk
London SE11 5HJ

This edition published 1994

10 9 8 7 6 5 4 3 2 1

© 1993 Anita Jeram

This book has been typeset
in Calligraphic 810.

Printed in Hong Kong

British Library Cataloguing
in Publication Data
A catalogue record for this
book is available from
the British Library.

ISBN 0-7445-3134-9

For all at the
special care Baby Unit,
RMH, Belfast

The Most Obedient Dog in the World

Anita Jeram

WALKER BOOKS
LONDON

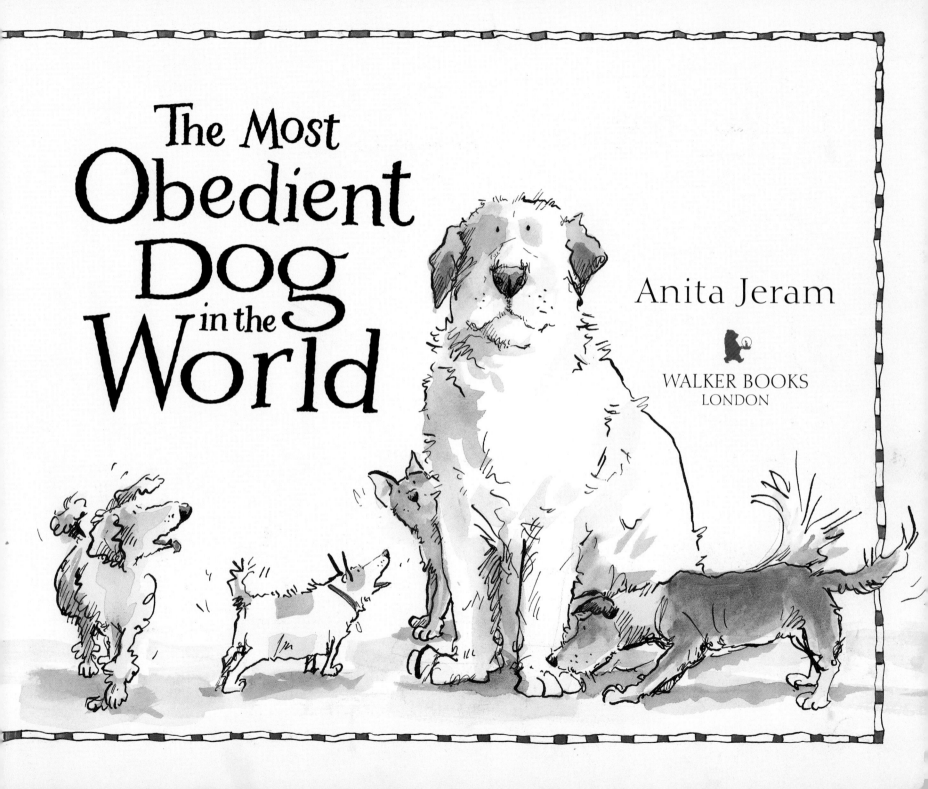

The most obedient dog in the world was
waiting for something to happen,

when Harry came up the path.

"Hello, boy," said Harry.

The most obedient dog in the world wagged
his tail and started to follow Harry.

"No ... sit!" said Harry. "I won't be long."
And then he was gone.

"Why are you sitting there?"
asked a nosy bird.

"Are you going to sit
there all day?"

The most obedient dog in the
world didn't answer.

He just sat and waited
for Harry.

Big, fat raindrops began to fall.

"I'm off," said the bird. And he flew away.

Everyone ran for cover, except
the most obedient dog
in the world.

Thunder rumbled, lightning flashed
and then the hailstones fell...

Quite a lot of hailstones!

When the sun came out again
the bird flew back. The most
obedient dog in the world
was still sitting there
waiting for Harry.

"What a strange dog," people said as they passed.

Other dogs came
to have a look.
They sniffed and
nuzzled and nudged
and nipped,

but they soon got bored
and went away.

The most obedient dog in the world sat ...

and sat ... and sat ... and sat.

How long must he wait for Harry?

Just then, a cat came by.

"Quick!" said the bird, pulling his tail.
"Why don't you chase it?"

The dog's eyes
followed the cat.
His nose started
to twitch,

and his legs started to itch.
He couldn't sit still
any longer.

He sprang to his feet ...

and saw Harry!

"Good boy!" said Harry. "You waited!
Leave that cat. Let's go to the beach!"

The dog looked at the cat, and he looked at Harry.

Then he went to the beach with Harry.

After all, he was ...

the most obedient dog in the world!

MORE WALKER PAPERBACKS
For You to Enjoy

IT WAS JAKE!
by Anita Jeram

Jake is a dog and he's Danny's special friend. He's also a useful scapegoat when Danny gets up to mischief!
This book is a National Curriculum SAT's reading list title.

"Full of humour ... great entertainment value. A fun book for parents
and toddlers to enjoy together." *Practical Parenting*

0-7445-2310-9   £3.99

BILL'S BELLY-BUTTON
by Anita Jeram

This is the enchanting story of an elephant who can't find his belly-button and the group of children who try to help him.

0-7445-2052-5   £3.99

WHEN I'M BIG
by Debi Gliori

A small child ponders the advantages of being big.

"Interprets every child's fears and ambitions... Debi Gliori's illustrations are full of humorous detail
which will find a wide audience among three and four year olds." *Valerie Bierman, The Scotsman*

0-7445-3125-X   £3.99

Walker Paperbacks are available from most booksellers, or by post from
Walker Books Ltd, PO Box 11, Falmouth, Cornwall TR10 9EN.

To order, send: Title, author, ISBN number and price for each book ordered, your full name and address,
cheque or postal order for the total amount, plus postage and packing:

UK and BFPO Customers – £1.00 for first book, plus 50p for the second book and plus 30p for each additional book to a maximum charge of £3.00.
Overseas and Eire Customers – £2.00 for first book, plus £1.00 for the second book and plus 50p per copy for each additional book.
Prices are correct at time of going to press, but are subject to change without notice.